"He's Your Dog, Charlie Brown!"

"He's Your Dog,"

Charlie Brown!"

by Charles M. Schulz

WORLD PUBLISHING
TIMES MIRROR
NEW YORK

Published by The World Publishing Company
110 East 59th Street, New York City, New York 10022
Published simultaneously in Canada
by Nelson, Foster & Scott Ltd.

1972 Printing

Copyright © 1968 by United Feature Syndicate, Inc.
Produced in association with
Lee Mendelson—Bill Melendez TV Production

Illustrations from the Lee Mendelson—Bill Melendez
television production "He's Your Dog, Charlie Brown!"

Library of Congress Catalog Card Number: 68-26838
ISBN: 0-529-04869-8

Printed in the United States of America

WORLD PUBLISHING
TIMES MIRROR

"He's Your Dog, Charlie Brown!"

What do you do when everyone in the neighborhood is complaining about your dog?

Snoopy had certainly been acting up lately, and the kids
were demanding that Charlie Brown do something about it.

"Why me?" he asked.

"Because he's your dog, Charlie Brown!"

That did it. Charlie Brown was forced into action, and he decided to write a letter to the Daisy Hill Puppy Farm.

DEAR DAISY HILL PUPPY FARM,
I AM WRITING IN REGARD
TO ONE OF YOUR LESS
DISTINGUISHED ALUMNI.

UNFORTUNATELY THIS
ALUMNUS IS NOT LIVING
UP TO MY EXPECTATIONS.
THEREFORE, I AM GOING TO
SEND HIM BACK AND HAVE YOU
TEACH HIM A LITTLE DISCIPLINE.

"This is for your own good, Snoopy, and don't look at me like that. You have no one to blame but yourself."

"Now, one other thing . . .
I'm going to call Peppermint
Patty and make arrangements
for you to spend the first
night at her house."

"Hello, Peppermint
Patty? Hi, this is 'Chuck,' you
know . . . 'Chuck' Brown . . .
Yeah . . . Well, I have a favor to
ask. Snoopy is going back to
school for a few days and he
needs a place to stay tonight.
Yeah, it's too far to make it in
one day. Can you put him up
for the night?"

"Sure, Chuck ... Glad to oblige."

Now, the weird thing about Peppermint Patty is that she somehow has never quite realized that Snoopy is a dog. She has always been impressed by Snoopy's baseball playing, and her enthusiasm has sort of blinded her.

They said good-by and Snoopy set off
with his dog dish on his head and carrying his
little suitcase. He was quite unhappy, a little
frightened, and very mad.

Snoopy was really
not in much of a hurry to
get where he was going,
so he meandered

down a few side streets,

kicked some tin cans,

and just took his time.

When he finally got to Peppermint Patty's house, he was greeted warmly.

"Hi, Snoopy, ol' pal! How's the ol' shortstop? It's good to see you again. Come on in, and I'll show you your room."

After Snoopy unpacked, Peppermint Patty fixed him a little snack in the kitchen. She was surprised when she saw him put his whole nose in a bowl of cereal. "This is the strangest kid I've ever seen," she thought to herself. But that was only the beginning.

     Now, Snoopy seated himself at a little table out in her backyard and really began to make a nuisance of himself. He leaned back in his chair and pretended that he was a World War I flying ace on leave in Paris, and he snapped his fingers for service just as if he were in a little sidewalk café. Peppermint Patty was too polite to say anything and she brought him a glass of root beer.

This went on for three days. Snoopy swam in the pool, sunned himself in the yard, and snapped his fingers whenever he wanted something.

Peppermint Patty was getting a little worried. The dishes in the sink were beginning to pile up, and she was getting tired of waiting on this guest who was taking unfair advantage of her good nature. "I'll have to call Charlie Brown," she said to herself.

"Hello, Chuck? I don't know about this friend of yours here. He seems to think he's on vacation or something. I thought he was supposed to go to school."

"You mean he's still there?" cried Charlie Brown. "I'll be right over and get him!"

Charlie Brown grabbed a leash and set off across town.
He hated the thought of putting a leash on Snoopy, but he
could see no other way of controlling this dog who had gotten
so out of hand.

And was Snoopy ever upset when Charlie Brown snapped the leash onto his collar and tried to drag him home!

Snoopy put on a wild performance pretending that the leash was strangling him. He coughed and he gasped, and he rolled on the ground.

Finally, he leaped to his feet, gave the leash a great yank
so that it flew from Charlie Brown's hand, and ran back to
Peppermint Patty's house.

"You're back again? Well, look, friend," said Peppermint Patty, "I'll let you stay awhile longer because I sort of like you, but let's get one thing straight. Around this house, everyone has to do his share. That's a family rule. You can stay with us if you want. You're perfectly welcome, but you're going to have to work! Did you hear me? Work!"

And Snoopy worked.
Peppermint Patty had him
doing dishes . . .

mowing grass . . .

washing windows . . .

vacuuming rugs . . . and taking
out the trash.

It wasn't long before Snoopy realized that he was caught between the leash and more work than he ever knew existed. And when he got careless and broke a dish, Peppermint Patty banished him to the garage for the night.

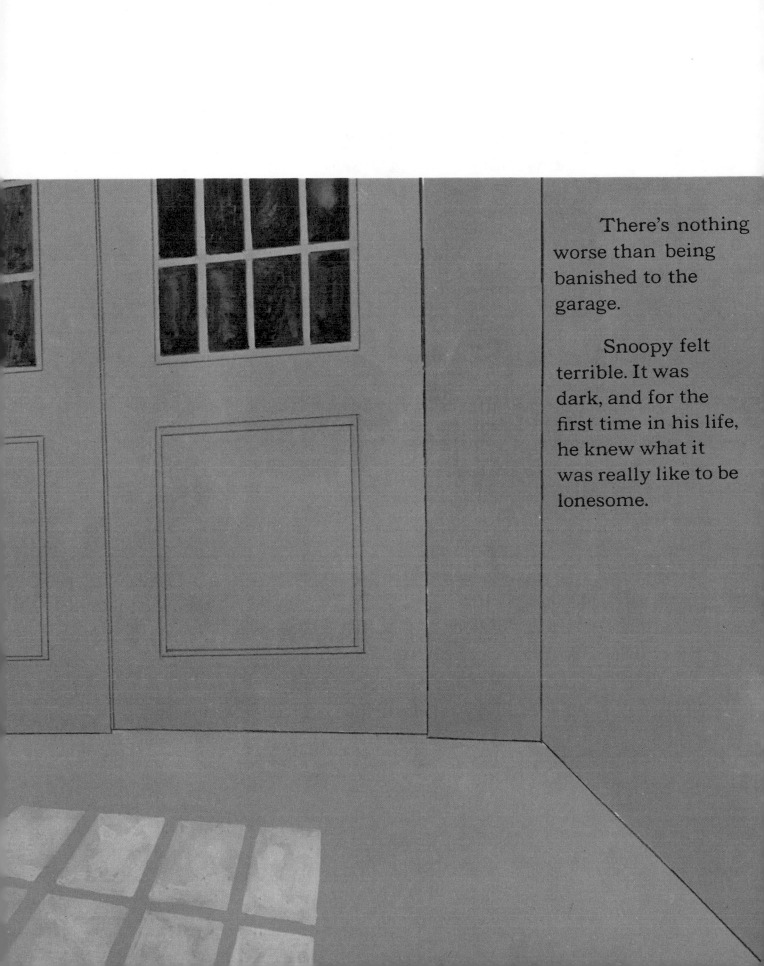

There's nothing worse than being banished to the garage.

Snoopy felt terrible. It was dark, and for the first time in his life, he knew what it was really like to be lonesome.

Fortunately, Peppermint
Patty had not locked the door,
so Snoopy was able to sneak
out, go into the house, gather all
his things together, and run
for home.

When Charlie Brown saw Snoopy at the front door, he
threw his arms in the air and grabbed him.

They danced around and around. And when they went to bed, Charlie Brown said, "It's good to have you back, Snoopy."

Of course, they had to compromise a little. Charlie Brown agreed not to send Snoopy away and Snoopy agreed to try to act a little less outrageously.

The next day, Snoopy realized he had learned a good lesson.

"When it comes right
down to it," he thought, as he
stretched out under the
bright blue sky, "dogs are born
to sleep in the sun."